THE KRYSTAL PRINCESSES™
SHAKE UP THE DAY

by Justine Korman
Illustrated by Jill Dubin

SCHOLASTIC INC.

New York   Toronto   London   Auckland   Sydney

ISBN 0-590-47881-8

12 11 10 9 8 7 6 5 4 3 2 1   3 4 5 6 7 8/9

Printed in the U.S.A.   24

First Scholastic printing, December 1993

Once upon a gloomy, gray day, a cloud formed high in the sky. But this cloud wasn't dark like a rain cloud. It was as pretty and pink as a tulip shining with dew. The cloud glowed from inside, like a sunny smile, because it was full of happy thoughts.

Of course, such a beautiful magical cloud couldn't rain ordinary, gloomy, gray rain. Each drop that fell from the glowing pink cloud contained a tiny princess as pretty as a perfect pearl.

Each princess's heart was filled with a happy thought.
And that happy thought shimmered around her in a shiny
Krystal dome. These lovely little princesses were the
Krystal Princesses.

The Krystal Princesses were very happy to have come out of their cloud. They danced and twirled their pretty gowns around them.

"I'm Princess Krystal Snow Dreams!" exclaimed one with hair as blue as the sky and eyes as bright as stars.

"I'm Princess Krystal Springtime!" cried another at the very same time.

All the other Krystal Princesses were chattering, too. Their voices sounded like the tinkling of tiny silver bells.

Princess Krystal Diamonds' mind was as bright and sharp as the jewels that floated in her Krystal dome. She was the smartest of the Krystal Princesses.

"Quiet, please!" Princess Krystal Diamonds said to her friends. "Let us act like the princesses that we are."

"How do princesses act?" wondered Princess Krystal Magic out loud. Her eyes were as mysterious as twin pools of moonlight.

"Yes, what are we supposed to do?" echoed pretty Princess Krystal Bows.

Princess Krystal Diamonds didn't know what to say. So she was glad when Princess Krystal Hearts replied, "I don't know what we're supposed to do. But I feel we have some purpose."

Princess Krystal Ballerinas twirled around the others in tiny circles. "I think our purpose is to dance!" she declared. "No! It's to flit and flutter and fly!" cried Princess Krystal Butterflies.

Princess Krystal Treats shook her silken hair. "We are here to make sweet treats to eat."

"But who are the treats for?" demanded Princess Krystal Springtime.

"I have a feeling they're not just for us," added Princess Krystal Hearts.

"Who else is there?" asked Princess Krystal Fairies, whose voice was as giddy as a giggle.

"Let's fly around and find out!" Princess Krystal Butterflies suggested.

But the princesses could not decide which way to fly.

Just then a sparrow flew up above the clouds. When he saw the tiny Krystal Princesses, the bird chirped and cheeped in amazement. He had never seen anything as beautiful.

"Who are you?" the bird asked.

"We are the Krystal Princesses," Princess Krystal
Diamonds replied.

"I'm Sparrow," chirped the brown bird. "I flew up here
to get away from the gloomy day."

"What's 'gloomy'?" asked one lovely princess.

"You know — ugly, sad, dull," the sparrow explained.

But the princesses knew nothing about ugly, sad, or dull, either.

As Sparrow explained about gloomy days and frowns and sad moods, Princess Krystal Hearts got an idea. She clapped her hands together and cried, "Now I know what we're supposed to do! We must bring happy thoughts to make people's hearts glad even on gloomy, gray days."

The other princesses thought that was a great idea. And so did Sparrow. So he showed them the way down through the clouds into the gloomy, gray day.

Soon the princesses found themselves flying over windswept
streets full of frowning people.

"We've got to do something!" declared Princess Krystal
Diamonds.

With a shake of their magic Krystals here and another
shake there, the Krystal Princesses spread happy thoughts
up and down the lane. Suddenly frowns turned into smiles,
and grumpy people started giggling.

"This is fun!" cried Princess Krystal Stars with excitement.
"Where would you like to go next?" asked Sparrow. The
flighty bird never stayed anywhere long enough for his
wings to get restless.

Princess Krystal Hearts looked thoughtful. "I have a feeling we should fly down this street," she said.

Sparrow shrugged his wings and said, "You should always follow your heart. Mine tells me there are many worms under that bush."

And with a cheery chirp and good-bye peck, he was gone.

The Krystal Princesses followed their hearts down one street and another. Soon they found themselves drawn to a cozy house in the middle of a quiet street. It looked like many of the other houses. But the princesses just knew someone special lived there.

And they were right! A little girl named Lindsay lived in the house. She was a very special girl indeed! She was the kind of girl who could dream the most beautiful daydream — even on gloomy, gray days. In fact, she was the very girl whose happy thoughts had brought the Krystal Princesses to life.

At first, Lindsay thought the twelve tiny princesses were just another daydream. But even Lindsay wasn't used to having her daydreams smile and wave at her.

Lindsay threw on her hat and coat and raced outside. She was afraid the lovely princesses would fade away like rainbows in the sun. But they were still there, and prettier up close.

When the Krystal Princesses introduced themselves, Lindsay's eyes grew wide with wonder.

"I know you!" she exclaimed. "You're all the happy thoughts that make even gloomy days bright."

The Krystal Princesses shook with delight. Happy thoughts swirled around them. Lindsay saw diamonds, hearts, flowers, fairies, ice cream cones, butterflies, ballerinas, bows, and snowflakes, too.

Then something magical happened. One of the snowflakes touched Lindsay's nose. And there was no mistaking the soft, cold, ticklish feeling of snow!

Lindsay looked up and saw thousands of tiny white flakes suddenly floating down from the clouds. The flakes swirled through the air, as if *they* were dancing with joy, too.